The Magic School Bus®
at the
First Thanksgiving

Arnold   Ralphie   Keesha   Phoebe   Carlos   Tim   Wanda   Dorothy Ann

SCHOLASTIC INC.

New York   Toronto   London   Auckland   Sydney
Mexico City   New Delhi   Hong Kong   Buenos Aires

Dear Parents,

Welcome to the Scholastic Reader series. We have taken over 80 years of experience with teachers, parents, and children and put it into a program that is designed to match your child's interests and skills.

Level 1—Short sentences and stories made up of words kids can sound out using their phonics skills and words that are important to remember.

Level 2—Longer sentences and stories with words kids need to know and new "big" words that they will want to know.

Level 3—From sentences to paragraphs to longer stories, these books have large "chunks" of text and are made up of a rich vocabulary.

Level 4—First chapter books with more words and fewer pictures.

It is important that children learn to read well enough to succeed in school and beyond. Here are ideas for reading this book with your child:

- Look at the book together. Encourage your child to read the title and make a prediction about the story.
- Read the book together. Encourage your child to sound out words when appropriate. When your child struggles, you can help by providing the word.
- Encourage your child to retell the story. This is a great way to check for comprehension.

Scholastic Readers are designed to support your child's efforts to learn how to read at every age and every stage. Enjoy helping your child learn to read and love to read.

> —**Francie Alexander**
> Chief Education Officer
> Scholastic Education

Ms. Frizzle

Liz

Written by Joanna Cole
Illustrated by Carolyn Bracken

Based on *The Magic School Bus* books
written by Joanna Cole and illustrated by Bruce Degen

ISBN-13: 978-0-439-89935-2
ISBN-10: 0-439-89935-4

12 11 10 9 8 7 6 5 4   40   10 11 12 13 14 15/0

Designed by Rick DeMonico

First printing, November 2006   Printed in the U.S.A.

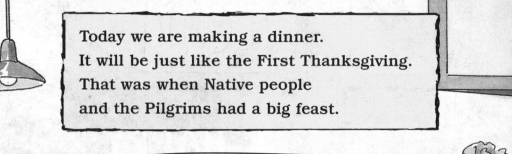

Today we are making a dinner.
It will be just like the First Thanksgiving.
That was when Native people
and the Pilgrims had a big feast.

THERE WAS A LOT OF FOOD AT THE FIRST THANKSGIVING.

THERE IS A LOT OF FOOD AT OUR THANKSGIVING.

WHO WERE THE NATIVE PEOPLE?
by Ralphie

They were a tribe that had lived in America for thousands of years.
The tribe was called the Wampanoag (say: Wam-pan-o-ag).

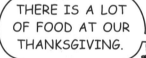

WHO WERE
THE PILGRIMS?
by Wanda

They were people who lived in England 400 years ago. Then, only one kind of church was allowed.

The Pilgrims wanted to worship God in their own way. So they left England and came to America.

We hop on the bus.
Then something happens.
The bus goes up in the air.
We go back in time.

We fly over the ocean.
We see a sailing ship.
The ship is the *Mayflower*.
It is carrying the Pilgrims.

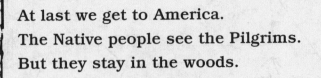

At last we get to America.
The Native people see the Pilgrims.
But they stay in the woods.

The Path of
the Mayflower
(Sept. 16, 1620 –
Nov. 21, 1620)

England
Europe

America

Africa

All winter, the Pilgrims are cold.
There is not much to eat.
Lots of Pilgrims get sick.
Many of them die.
WINTER CAN BE HARD.
LET'S KEEP THIS FIRE GOING.

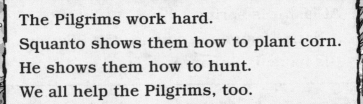

The Pilgrims work hard.
Squanto shows them how to plant corn.
He shows them how to hunt.
We all help the Pilgrims, too.

SQUANTO KNOWS A LOT ABOUT LIVING IN AMERICA.

When fall comes, there are
seven new houses.
And there is a lot of food.
The Pilgrims save food for the winter.

MAKING CORN BREAD

WE'RE THANKFUL FOR THAT!

DRYING SQUASH

The Pilgrims plan a celebration.
They cook food.
They set up tables.
Everyone works—even the children.

DIGGING CLAMS

CUTTING UP EELS

TURNING THE SPIT

We get a surprise.
A Native chief comes.
He brings many people.
Will there be enough to eat?

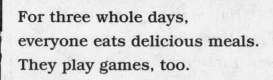

For three whole days,
everyone eats delicious meals.
They play games, too.

BLINDMAN'S BUFF

THIS IS FUN!

RING AND PIN

Ms. Frizzle says it is time to go.
We say good-bye to our new friends.

HOW THE PILGRIMS' THANKSGIVING WAS DIFFERENT FROM OURS

Theirs	Ours
The Pilgrims did not call their feast "Thanksgiving." It was a celebration. They thanked God on other days. On those days, they didn't eat at all. They just prayed.	Today our Thanksgiving is a feast *and* a day to give thanks.
Theirs lasted for three days.	Ours lasts only one day.
Theirs was in October in 1621.	Ours is in November every year.
Theirs included boiled pumpkin.	Ours includes pumpkin pie.

In 1863, President Abraham Lincoln
made Thanksgiving a national holiday.